DAHLIA

Barbara McClintock

Frances Foster Books   Farrar, Straus and Giroux   New York

IT WAS a beautiful blue morning. Charlotte and Bruno were making mud cakes when Charlotte's mother called.

There was a package for Charlotte. Inside was a doll. Her painted mouth was prim. She was dressed in linen and lace and delicate silk ribbons. Frail hands were covered with thin gloves.

Charlotte found a note. "Dear Charlotte, I saw this doll and thought of you. Tell your mother I'm coming for dinner. Love, Aunt Edme."

Charlotte didn't have a doll. Charlotte didn't want a doll. She carried the doll upstairs, thinking at any moment it might break.

In Charlotte's room, among the dragonflies and boxes of beetles and found birds' nests, the doll looked out of place.

"We like digging in dirt and climbing trees," Charlotte confessed to the doll. "No tea parties, no being pushed around in frilly prams. You'll just have to get used to the way we do things."

The doll looked concerned, but said nothing.

Bruno and the doll were lowered
down in a basket from the bedroom
window.

Charlotte climbed after them.

They finished making mud cakes. The doll tasted one. She seemed to like it!

Charlotte and Bruno made boats from sticks and leaves and sailed them down the stream. The doll looked on with pleasure, Charlotte thought.

To Charlotte and Bruno's surprise, the doll took to fishing very well.

When Charlotte wiped the doll's face dry, her painted mouth blurred into a soft smile.

They dug in the flower bed, planting many small stones. "You look like one of Mother's flowers. Dahlia! That's a perfect name for you." Dahlia looked back brightly.

Dahlia eagerly joined in Bruno's favorite game of toss-up-in-the-air-and-land-in-a-heap. Her cheeks and chin grew brown and warm. The exercise seemed to do her good.

Dahlia sat next to Bruno in his wagon, and Charlotte took them for a ride. "You're not jealous, are you, Bruno?" whispered Charlotte. Bruno didn't mind at all.

At the top of the hill, a cluster of boys stood with their wagons, ready for a race.

"We'll race, too," said Charlotte.

"With a doll?" snickered George.

"Dressed in lace?" snorted Paul.

"She's braver than all of you," said Charlotte.

Dahlia raised her chin slightly, ready for the challenge.

One, two, three~the race began!
Dahlia sat in front, bumping up
and down, hair blown back.
They won!

Dahlia, Bruno, and Charlotte accepted the grand prize of a cracked but handsome cup. After saying thank you, they headed home.

Oh, splendid day! They still had time to climb Charlotte's favorite tree.

Up they went, Bruno in one pocket, Dahlia in the other,
higher than they really should have gone.

Dahlia sat far out on the branch,
to have a better view.

Perhaps it was the wind.
Maybe Dahlia sneezed.
   She leaned too far over,
and fell down, down, and
landed hard on the ground.
   "Dahlia!"

Charlotte and Bruno climbed down. There she lay, lace and ribbons crumpled and torn. She smiled a little, not wanting to worry Charlotte too much. Charlotte grasped Dahlia and held her close.

"Poor Dahlia," Charlotte wept. "My poor Dahlia."

Charlotte ran all the way home, Bruno cradling Dahlia in the wagon bumping behind.

What to do? Charlotte got out bandages and a bowl of warm water and plenty of towels.

She bathed Dahlia and bandaged her arms and legs and put her to bed.

Bruno held Dahlia's hand while Charlotte read softly from her favorite book.

Finally, Dahlia's eyes opened. She felt good as new!

Charlotte brushed Dahlia's hair and straightened her dress.

She brushed Bruno, too.

"And I'd better do the same."

Downstairs, a door opened. There were voices in the hall.
"Charlotte! Your Aunt Edme is here!"

"Quickly! It's time to go down," whispered Charlotte.

There was Aunt Edme, frail hands folded in her lap. She was wearing lace and linen and silk ribbons, looking just the way Dahlia had in her box that morning.

"Charlotte, dear! How do you like your new doll?" asked Aunt Edme.

"I~Bruno and I~like her very much. She has become our best friend," said Charlotte.

"May I see the doll?" asked Aunt Edme.

Charlotte held Dahlia up for Aunt Edme to see. She was muddy and torn, her hair tangled in knots, but her face was softened into a sweet, warm smile. Aunt Edme studied the doll . . . then . . .

Aunt Edme smiled, too!

"When I saw your doll in a shop window, I thought she needed to be out in the sunshine, and played with, and loved. I knew that is just what you would do for her. I only wish I could make mud pies and be tossed in the air, but I'm too old."

Aunt Edme kissed Charlotte and Dahlia on the cheek. She shook Bruno's paw.

From then on, Dahlia made mud cakes and climbed trees and rode with Bruno and was loved by Charlotte, for ever after.

To the Chandoha family,
Kyra Grace Noonan, and,
as always, to Larson

Distributed in Canada by Douglas & McIntyre Ltd.
Color separations by Hong Kong Scanner Arts
Printed in the United States of America by Berryville Graphics
Interior designed by Filomena Tuosto
Jacket designed by Nancy Goldenberg
First edition, 2002
1 3 5 7 9 10 8 6 4 2

Library of Congress Cataloging-in-Publication Data
McClintock, Barbara.
  Dahlia / Barbara McClintock.– 1st ed.
      p. cm.
  Summary: Charlotte does not like dolls, until she receives a special
doll from her aunt and they become good friends.
  ISBN 0-374-31678-3
  [1. Dolls–Fiction. 2. Toys–Fiction.] I. Title.

PZ7.M1332 Dah 2002
[E]–dc21

                                                              2001018778